Zlebra Family Secrets

LILLIE JOHNSON

authorHOUSE®

AuthorHouse™
1663 Liberty Drive
Bloomington, IN 47403
www.authorhouse.com
Phone: 833-262-8899

This is a work of fiction. All of the characters, names, incidents, organizations, and dialogue in this novel are either the products of the author's imagination or are used fictitiously.

Published by AuthorHouse 01/27/2021

ISBN: 978-1-6655-1545-0 (sc)
ISBN: 978-1-6655-1552-8 (e)

Print information available on the last page.

This book is printed on acid-free paper.

Scripture quotations marked KJV are from the Holy Bible, King James Version (Authorized Version). First published in 1611. Quoted from the KJV Classic Reference Bible, Copyright © 1983 by The Zondervan Corporation.

CONTENTS

PREFACE

When I was younger, I didn't know if I wanted to be a photographer or a preacher. I liked taking pictures, but I wanted to whoop and holler. God blessed me, however, with a gift to write, and I enjoy and love writing.

My family lived on seventeen acres of land, surrounded by trees. I didn't realize the beauty of it until I was grown and everything had changed back home. We had three houses—my brother Leroy's (we called him Dula) house, Robert Lee's house, and our old wooden shack. About twenty or thirty feet from our back door was the potato house; my brother Clarence (we called him Son) lived there. When Robert Lee moved to Texas, we moved into his house—I was eleven then—and Son moved into our shack.

When we moved, we finally had indoor plumbing—no more having to sit on that oil bucket at night because I couldn't go to the toilet down the hill. My own room had two nice-sized windows. The house had a den and green concrete steps, shaped in the form of three wide smiles. I couldn't believe all the furniture and things that filled that green house, from the living room to the den and all the other rooms in between. I enjoyed playing on the carport on rainy days. Nothing compared to that cozy home.

I remember Daddy going into the fields. We kids would pick blackberries and put them in a milk jug or ice cream buckets. Mama would make pies or dumplings. I ate only the dumplings; I didn't like blackberries.

Daddy made a swing for me—rope and a piece of board—between three trees, facing the window to the living room, which also was Mom and Dad's room. I remember days of Daddy cutting the grass in the yard, with the sun yellowish-orange and the wind sharing its fragrance of lightly wet grass through the screens on the window; it made me feel peaceful. Daddy and Dula went into the woods to put an electric fence around the pigpen so that the wild dogs that came out at night wouldn't kill the pigs.

I would hold on to a vine and swing back and forth. My view was so clean and clear and amazingly breathtaking.

I got a lot of hand-me-downs. I couldn't wait for Mr. Jim to bring those black garbage bags with clothes in them—I'd be so excited. Mrs. Willie Mae, from up the road, also gave me clothes. We were poor, but I didn't know it.

Mom did not let us watch our floor-model Zenith TV all the time. I would come home from school and watch thirty minutes of *Batman: The Animated Series*. Then I'd head outside. We played with whatever we had. We would make teams and throw bicycle wheels. We had to get out of the way or get hit. We'd play a game that I called "Sticks" to see how far we could jump. In the backyard, we'd get on an L-shaped dolly and push ourselves down the hill. Then we'd jump off before it hit the outhouse; no one got hurt. We also enjoyed raking leaves and throwing them in the air or burning them. Along with the sweet potatoes. We played hopscotch, and I'd hope to be the one to win the game by marking an X in the number-ten spot. We played kickball in the front yard—or "kill a man with the ball."

We drank water from a rusty red pump, using an aluminum dipper. That made all the difference on a hot day. Later, we got an electric pump, but when it broke, we had to fill buckets and empty milk jugs with water from Dula's—that seemed to be the longest walk ever.

I never realized how blessed we were and how beautiful everything was, including Mom's garden and that big old tree. I would sit on its roots, put my feet in the sunken hole, and think. Robert Lee had an old, rusty yellow tractor sitting outside the fence, and that tree had a hole that was filled with bees. I think my brother Henry got stung; I know I did, and I was not the one who was throwing rocks at the bees.

When Daddy came home, he would park his truck on the side of the house by the two butane tanks. Ours was the round tank, and Robert Lee's was really long. After we moved into Robert Lee's house, we had a phone installed—that was big news. It meant we didn't have to go to Mrs. Mary and Mr. Frank's to make a call; they were nice. I liked dialing that old black rotary phone and listening to the sound it made.

My nephew Jeff, who was Robert Lee's son, had a white dog named King. Some days when I played in the yard, King would get out of the fenced yard and chase me back in the house. I was the only kid who King chased like that. Mom had a golden-tan-and-white guinea pig named Della. Mom took a picture with Della one day.

During the evening, Mom often made jumbo popcorn balls.

On hot days, my brothers and I would go to the creek to cool off. If the day was hot enough, the tar on the blacktop road would bubble, and I'd go to the top of the road, take off my shoes, and pop those bubbles with my toe. I could only go as far up the road as where the mailboxes were located.

I have so many other beautiful memories, including seeing the pumpkins and watermelons growing by the edge of the trash pile.

We lived for ten years in that three-room shack. A wisteria vine had twisted itself around the corner of the porch. Sometimes, Mama would make breakfast food for dinner—old-fashioned bacon with the rind on it, homemade syrup and biscuits, and eggs; it was the best breakfast ever.

I remember my cousin Froggy bringing sugarcane over in the evening as a treat. I didn't like it; silly me—I preferred sweet grass. Froggy gave me my first bicycle; it had training wheels and was dark blue with black tape around it, like a candy cane. My brother Herman tried to teach me to ride it, but I would look at the pedals.

Some days, Mama plaited my hair and greased my scalp with Blue Magic Conditioner, a type of hair grease. She would wear beige polyester pants, cut off just below her knees, and a light-green blouse as she stood before a big dishpan. She'd make hog's head cheese or five-layer cakes for the holidays. For each of my birthdays, until I was eleven, Mama would get two coconut cakes from Winn-Dixie. Each one had a cherry on top, and Mama put the cakes on the table on the porch. I enjoyed eating the cake, even though I didn't like coconut cake; her love is what made it taste good.

In the winter, Daddy would get our old heater and put it in the living room; it went through the roof, and we could cook on it.

I would have traded the indoor plumbing for that outhouse, and I'd have taken that three-room shack over all the rooms in our new house, with its fenced yard and rainy-day carport. I took multiple pictures in front of the tree that stood in the corner of the fence, by the clothesline in the backyard. My birthday fireworks were placed on those clothes poles, and a garden of colors exploded in the night sky that surrounded Mama's garden, which Dad made for her.

In December 1983, death's door opened for my daddy to walk through, and ten months later, because of her broken heart, Mama followed. They had been together for more than forty years. I would take a thousand days times a million to live in that shack with my loving parents again. I know that when we lived in that shack, I did not get the short end of the stick; rather, I got the gift of imagination. That old three-room shack wasn't bad; it was years of having few material things, but we were enriched so much more by God's beautiful blessings—the gift of old parents, who had morals and who taught God's Word and the value of an honest day's work, whether in your own field or on someone's clock.

As I write this, I sit here with tears in my eyes. I can see Mama biting a plug from Day's Work tobacco, and Daddy sitting by the heater, with his white socks on, smoking his pipe or Salem cigarettes'. I am thankful that I have seen God's beautiful blessings from my past and presence.

Whether you are on several acres of land or just passing by a park or a tree or two, I hope you open your eyes and enjoy God's beauty in nature and in all forms of life. God bless you.

CHAPTER 1

Beauty's Beginnings

Mr. Kend Zlebra did not own the town, but he was from one of the richest families in Goose Burn and had enough money to buy it and several towns connected to it—and several more that were farther out.

My story takes place in springtime, and that makes me think of the east garden, the prettiest of the four gardens; it was the one I cared for. It was filled with birds of all kinds, butterflies, flowers, and other plants, such as wisteria, roses, golden daffodils, lilies of the valley, and—my favorite—English bluebells. I hoped that when I died, I would be surrounded by English bluebells—and so many others, creatures hidden and seen. The east garden made me wonder how beautiful the garden of Eden was.

There were beautiful ponds with golden bridges and engraved

handprints on the railings, if you needed a grip to cross. There also were lakes and man-made miniature waterfalls, hills, carpets of green, oversized colorful windmills, fruit trees, and vegetable gardens. Zlebra had several gold-painted, glistening, log-cabin water wheels that were simply amazing on sunny days. There were lots of horses, and at certain times of the year, Zlebra had exotic animals as well; then, the next day, all of them would be gone—I did not know why or how. The land itself was mesmerizing. In the center of the numerous acres of land was the Zlebras' enormous mansion. Looking at this beauty from the outside, you might think it was heaven on earth. But although he had everything he desired, Zlebra—or Mr. Z, as he was known—was truly empty inside.

Few of us knew the seeds of torment or the fatal stamen within its petals.

Kendrick, the Zlebras' son, was always off to a boarding school or training camp—his father's cruel punishment because Kendrick loved taking pictures and recording music. As smart as Mr. Z was, he believed that cameras captured one's soul. There were no pictures of Mr. Z anywhere in the mansion. Maybe there had been a photo of him at some point, or maybe there never was one because he didn't want his darkness seen. Lord knows I saw a lifetime of his evil.

Mrs. Frances Zlebra was tall and thin with an angular face; Mr. Z said it was diamond-shaped, "for the jewel she is." Mrs. Z would stand by the north gate with the wind blowing through the fiery waves of her long hair. Her voice was hoarse but sweet and gentle, like her warm smile. At noon, I would bring her fresh apple cider that I had made earlier that morning from the apples I picked from one of the trees I'd planted years ago. She never wanted lemonade or iced tea. A kind soul—that was the picture I saw; an angel, more like it. I wondered how she and Mr. Z came to be married. She was nothing like him. When he came home from one of his many trips, I would have the Roamer two-seater ready for him to take Mrs. Z around the track a few times, and I'd see that beautiful, fiery hair disappearing and reappearing, dancing within the wind.

Kendrick was not a junior because Mr. Zlebra said that Kendrick had to earn his name. He went away to college. His was the only birth that was granted to Mrs. Z's womb at the age of fortysomething. He had his mother's deep-emerald eyes and kindness but a round face, like Mr. Z's, and with the same medium build, long arms, and broad shoulders—handsome, some would say. His hair was golden, with thick locks, like his dad's. He had a laugh so loud that if you ever heard it, you would jump out of your skin.

I taught Kendrick to ride his first bike, to drive a car, and to swim. He was a child filled with wonder when it came to learning and with compassion and a troubled heart for poor people.

Mr. Z was a different ball game; he was hateful, mean, boastful, and evil, inside and out. Everyone knew about his love for cars; he treated them better than his help. His large garage would never be filled because he always was adding more space to it. When he bought a car, he paraded through town in it to show off. That was for the people who didn't get to see the cars when they were delivered—three new ones, the same color, every year for the past several decades. He and his rich friends would swap cars. The sports cars would race around a seven-mile track—"that happy track," as Mr. Z and his friends called it. Truth be told, it was Satan's torture track. I knew every inch of those seven miles because tending to the track was another of the chores I performed myself, along with keeping those cars clean and running.

I thought of the hungry stomachs that could have been filled for a long time for the value of just one car. Mr. Z, however, would have watched the cars burn before helping those he thought were less important.

CHAPTER 2

I Am God!

I taught Kendrick how to be gentle with the horses and how to fish, plant, and do many other things his dad did not think were important. I was his best "nigger"—that came from Mr. Z's mouth all the time: a wonder-working, man-made machine; his trusted A. N. ("advanced nigger"). I was smarter than all the other help—a lot of the pure white folk too—but not smarter than Mr. Z. Those are words I would never repeat.

Once, when the mechanic couldn't fix one of his cars, Mr. Z said, "I'll buy another one."

"Could I take a look at it?" I asked.

"Sure," he said.

I took apart took his Durant Model A-22, piece by piece, and fixed it that December—that was how I earned my name, A. N., not that he'd ever called me Edgar. That didn't bother me. I was a nobody in Mr. Z's eyes, but for Kendrick, I was an ear to listen to his hurt and a heart to understand, with wisdom to know that all the money Mr. Z had could not fill his son's empty well of love that he needed from his father.

I held Kendrick's hand more than his dad, and during difficult times, he cried on my shoulder. He was respectful all the time, even though it made Mr. Z furious because I was lower than a dog----definitely not a man. the help were not important. We were creatures who were disposable to the white man and used for whatever he needed us to do.

Mr. Z would look at me and say with a laugh, "You are the only mistake God made."

When things did not go smoothly for Mr. Z, I had to listen and not speak as he ranted. If I ever repeated what went on in the Zlebras' home or anything associated with the Zlebra name, Mr. Z would have the blood beat from me. He would do that whenever he wanted, at any time, but mostly before the break of dawn, saying, "A good beating will make you work better."

I thought of all the beatings and torture that I got from him and his friends; none of them were good men.

Working for him, he said, meant *he* owned our souls, not God.

Evil was the blood in his veins. He was not afraid of life or death.

He hired only young Negroes, Mexicans, and Puerto Ricans whose

families couldn't pay their debts. We became his property, never

seeing our families unless it was for the rich folks' entertainment.

We did not want to see them at all because if we got out of line,

our families would be tortured in front of us—and worse. We

could not escape him any more than we could have escaped our

shadows. Our only reprieve was old age and being buried in the

east garden, which welcomed its tortured mules home.

You might think that because Mr. Z was surrounded by all

this beauty, a little of it would have seeped into even his darkened

heart, but no—not his.

He was an arrogant genius. Everything he touched flourished,

including his evil deeds toward those who were less important.

Before he left on each trip, he told his help, "I will know if you

look the wrong way or do something that is not pleasing or if a

foolish thought enters your mind."

Sometimes, we did fear him more than God. How could one

man own that much land, as far as the eye could see, and not make

himself a god? That's what Mr. Z thought he was.

He said he had the best of everything—dwellings, attorneys, automobiles, friends, neighbors. He once looked me in my face, laughed, and shouted, "Slaves too." He then asked me, "You know what *having it all* means?"

"No, sir, Mr. Z," I said with a smile.

"Pure power, that's what it takes. Look at my niggers—nothing but the best, after I whip them into shape. Work better than any goddamn Belgian draft horse or any animal. My creatures do what I make them do." Laughing louder, he added, "You know I am right."

The things we servants went through before he paid off our family debts! Some did not make it and are buried at the east garden. And the debt did not get paid unless they had more deserving family members (mules) who would be their replacements.

It makes me feel mad, sad, and useless that I will never have children or grandchildren. Mr. Z had all the male servants "fixed" by Dr. Manning, like one of his projects. Many of us were taken before the tender age of ten years old—children being placed in men's slavery shoes. You had to catch on quickly or be beaten and suffer slowly as you were dragged around Satan's track. For countless souls, I prayed that death would open its doors speedily.

They were surrounded by all the other help as they were used as examples to us.

When that black cloud of hate was in Mr. Z's heart and above his head, his friends were there too, as were some of the mothers and sisters of the slaves, telling them they better run around that track fast as hell. Then, he let the dogs tear them to shreds as he laughed. I cried along with my brothers, as if it was my mother or sister being tortured. His men would burn the fathers or brothers, cut their private areas, and pour hot tar on them. They beat them with boards, iron, or whatever they thought made it funny or entertaining. These white devils were sober but drunk with laughter and its attached willful, hungry stupidity. So many were dragged by their necks, limbs, or whatever flesh they could grasp around that seven-mile track. I still have nightmares about to this day. I had to clean the blood that penetrated blood that endless track. It didn't matter if we were black, brown, or red; we were all the same.

Mr. Z did not want us talking among ourselves, so we had little words we used between us. There was a lot of hurt, anger, and pain, combined with mountains of fear. We shared it all silently, keeping it within, too ignorant to do anything about it.

CHAPTER 3

Forbidden Roots

When rich white people moved to Goose Burn, Mr. Z would see that they had the best help, even if it tore poor families apart. I met only one family out of hundreds—the Purses—who I thought were okay in my heart. They did not belong with the other people in town; they were different—kind.

The Jewels were neighbors whose house was hidden among the trees. They were rich, like the thickness of black tar, but hateful and terrifying. The Purses were a wonderful family—rich but "tainted," Mr. Z would say, because his nephew Thomas had slept with their daughter, Sarah, and she had a child—a boy who couldn't carry the Zlebra name because the child wasn't pure. He came out dark, and the doctor said he was "mixed breed, worse than a mutt." Mr. Z had wanted his nephew's child to be terminated, but the Purses were white, so they said that the child had to be placed for adoption. That friendship ended in that second.

It should have been a blessing to the Purses, getting away from those devils. Mr. Z had the townspeople harass the Purses until they moved; their daughter, Sarah, stayed behind because she was in love. Thomas didn't want to be disinherited from the family fortune, so he lied to her, saying they would get married, but the baby had to be baptized by the priest first.

Sarah knew she couldn't attend. Her love for Thomas led her to a lifetime of tears for the loss of her infant son. Thomas placed the baby in her arms and walked away without a word because, rich or not, if you're not pure, you're the same as the help. Sarah called her dad to come to get her—and she was never seen again.

That was the spring that the garden's blossoms didn't open, and winter's cold skeleton shadowed the garden that entire rainy season. I'd taken the child from her frail arms, broken heart, and lifeless eyes and called him Miraculous because he wasn't tainted by the evils of Mr. Z. If the child had lived, Mr. Z would have had Miraculous beaten daily or dragged around that track. I buried him beneath the rainbow tulips and next to the field of blue roses, which were saluted by the lilies of the valley. I prayed to the only God and cried with thankfulness for this angel, who was going home to live with God.

Three months later, Thomas married Ms. Debra, the Jewels' youngest girl, in a wedding only Mr. Z could put together so quickly. They went on to have two girls and Thomas Jr., who was the training-wheel twin of Mr. Z. When Thomas came by, he dropped off Thomas Jr. for the weekend. He never visited Miraculous's grave, nor did he even glimpse in that direction—not that it mattered because he chose murder and greed over love. Two murders took place in that spring of 1922. Sarah died the second Thomas handed her Miraculous and walked away.

CHAPTER 4

Dinner Is Canceled

Winter came and then let go so spring could beautify the earth that the ice had smothered and let it breathe again.

Mr. Kendrick was home from his schooling and had a surprise.

At suppertime, Mrs. Z sat at the dinner table, the candlelight reflecting in her hair. She was as lovely as always and seemed to get prettier with time.

"Doorbell!" I called out and ran to open the door. There stood Mr. Kendrick with a woman. "Let me take your hat," I said to him in greeting.

Instead, the woman handed me her purse to put away until after supper. As I reached for it, my hand brushed against her smooth, silky caramel skin. I stared at her briefly. Then I showed them to the dining room and pulled out her chair so she could sit.

"Father, Mother," Kendrick said as he took his seat, "may I introduce your beautiful daughter-in-law, Rose Zlebra."

"Son, let's talk in my study."

I do not know what dropped to the floor first Mr. Z's napkin or his jaw. He got up quickly but still was too slow. His son brought home a bronze beauty.

I glanced at Mrs. Z from the corner of my eye. She smiled.

"Son," Mr. Z said, raising his voice, "my study—now!"

"Father, there is no need to go to your study."

For a second, Kendrick seemed to forget how his father was when he demanded going to his study. "Yes, sir." He got up and kissed Ms. Rose on her glowing cheek. "Father, she's a God-fearing woman."

"I think she is lovely," Mrs. Z said, grabbing Mr. Z's hand and whispering something in his ear.

Mr. Z looked at Ms. Rose with a stupid grin.

"I met her in college," Kendrick explained.

"We know that, but this marriage thing is serious," Mr. Z said.

"I love her, Father, and refuse to let her go for any reason."

"Is she in trouble?"

"No, Father. I respect her; she's a lady. I didn't touch her until we were married. Like you and Mother, we were both virgins."

If I had been in the garden or even in town, I would have heard Mr. Z when he bellowed, "Edgar! Edgar!"

That was the first time he used my name. I didn't know that he remembered it, as I hadn't heard him use it in sixty-some years. I also didn't know Mr. Z could get up from the table like a mongoose after a snake. Boy, did I chuckle inside, and it felt so good.

The closer I got to the wine cellar, the louder my chuckle became. My soul was showered with laughter and sadness because I didn't know what kind of evil Mr. Z would do. I got his extra-strong drink that he had flown in from Europe. He claimed it calmed him and put him to sleep, even though the next day, he would be meaner than a rattlesnake.

"Mr. Kend, let me show them to their room," I suggested.

"No, you take … uh, what did he say her name was? I'm sorry—haven't been feeling myself," he said.

I chuckled inside again "What seems to be the matter, Mr.

Kend?" I turned to his wife. "Mrs. Z, do you need me to get anything?"

She shook her head. "That will be all. Show Rose to their room in the east wing."

"Yes, ma'am. Good night. Ms. Rose, I will bring you something to eat. Is there anything special you prefer?"

She looked at me with starry brown eyes. When she smiled, deep dimples creased her cheeks. "If you wouldn't mind, a warm bowl of oatmeal and a glass of milk."

"Sure." That reminded me of the sleepless nights when Kendrick ate warm oatmeal while he waited for his dad to come home.

I brought the oatmeal to Ms. Rose, knocking on the door.

"Come in, Edgar. Thank you so much." She kissed my cheek and hugged me good night.

This old soul had a trail of tears from my heart. After making it downstairs, I put my head to the study door to listen to Mr. Z's conversation with his son.

"Son, she looks like the help," I heard him say. "How could you marry her. How do you know she was pure?"

"Father, she was a virgin. She is all I need. I love her. I want her to have our babies—your grandchildren."

"I don't think you know what I mean when I say *pure*."

"I love her, Father. Mother, I love her."

"Be happy, son," Mrs. Z said. "Your Father and I have to take care of some business, and we need to pack. Give me a hug. All is well. Go be with your bride, and let her know we are happy to have her. Love you, son. Let me talk with your father. We'll see you in the morning."

I hurried to the kitchen and stood by the pantry.

"Edgar!" Kendrick called out.

"Yeah, son?"

"Thanks for everything."

"Good night, Kendrick."

As I was checking the lights and doors before bed, I passed by Mr. Kend's bedroom and overheard Mrs. Z talking.

"Honey, she has a tan. We don't want another Sarah—no darkies. Anyway, how could she afford to attend the same college as Kendrick? Those types of people have to pay triple to attend, and then they are in the basement, not learning what the smarter white kids are. Have you forgotten what I whispered in your ear?"

"No darkies allowed, ever!"

"I did not."

"We have enough of the help to look at. When I think about Edgar, his black tar-baby self, it makes my skin crawl. How could God make something that black?"

"I don't want nigger grandbabies."

"You let him know by tomorrow evening—if he doesn't get his mind right about her, we will have Dr. Manning fix her— permanently! Let him know he will not get one red cent from us. He will have to leave the estate immediately if he doesn't agree with us. You know I have a plan."

"That's why I love my green-eyed angel so much, keeping the circle pure. I'm tired. You know how that leopard's blood affects me. Let's get some sleep."

I could not believe that the woman I thought was an angel was the devil herself—fake eyes, fake smile, fake everything. I hoped that when she was outside, the wind would blow her hair so hard that it would get tangled around her neck or that it would get caught in a tire wheel and pull her around that happy track.

Poor Kendrick—how could so much hate bring forth a child to grow in love.

Mr. Z wanted Kendrick to help him cut some sugarcane because he always cut it himself. Kendrick was grown now; maybe he could help.

CHAPTER 5

Betrayal Continues

The next morning, Mr. and Mrs. Z planned the day for Rose and Kendrick. At that point, I didn't know what was going on, but I knew what I'd heard, and I decided to keep my eyes and ears on Mr. and Mrs. Z.

I went upstairs and saw Mrs. Z's luggage. I accidently knocked one over as she came into the room. "Traveling light?" I asked.

"These are my personal things. I'm not finished packing," she said. "Mr. Z will take our luggage to the car. And when did you start weighing luggage?" She rudely escorted me out and closed her door but not before saying, "Thank you."

I didn't get a chance to talk to Kendrick, but when I went to the stables to brush the horse's mane, I couldn't get Rose out of my mind. I felt I knew her, but I did not know her at all. I had met her for the first time the previous evening.

I don't go through people's things, but I went to the east wing and tidied up the room a bit. That's when I saw a picture in the drawer under their wedding papers. I could not believe it; they knew who she was from the moment Kendrick had introduced her to them. I prayed that Lord would keep them safe.

I went to the east garden, crying, and knelt next to where I'd buried Miraculous, in his perfect spot.

Lord, they knew.

I knew every tunnel, hidden road, and secret place at the Zlebra estate. There were so many.

One winter night, when I couldn't sleep, I heard sounds that I could not understand. It was eerie, so I decided to go through the tunnel, heading north. Boy, was I surprised and sickened by the things I saw them doing to those animals. I knew these rich people were beyond evil; they were having sex with the animals and then killing them and eating them raw. Every tunnel was filled with darkness.

Mr. Z and all his rich friends will burn in hell, I'd thought. *Thank God that Mrs. Z doesn't do these things.* It looked like it was just the menfolk; they were all in black gowns or robes with hoods and shining gold on their faces. I got the hell out of there and did not let them see me, but I'll never forget it.

Into the stables I went and through the underground tunnel that led to the road. I waited for Kendrick to come home, and I flagged him down.

"Kendrick, will you and Rose attend the church meeting and later attend the banquet for the poor?"

Kendrick looked in my eyes, grabbed my arm, and said, "I have always trusted you, Edgar."

Rose smiled at me with those deep dimples and said, "You remind me of my uncle who passed before I was born. My great-grandmother Sarah would tell stories of my uncle Albert, who worked in a mansion. I could picture him in my heart—a kind, gentle soul who experienced endless mistreatment and disappointment until the angels called him home. I pray that you will have your flowers of joy in this lifetime. When you opened the door as we arrived last night, it took me back to when I would sit on the porch, rubbing my great-grandmother's swollen, tired feet. She would look toward the heavens and smile when talking about Uncle Albert."

I slightly smiled at Rose and said, "You two hurry. If possible, stay overnight at Reverend Clyde's house. Hurry, you two."

I went back the way I'd come. I was not worried much about Kendrick and Ms. Rose, but the mountain of trouble for Mr. and Mrs. Z was building—or the grave holes they were digging for someone to fall in were deepening.

The next evening, I was in the kitchen, just thinking.

Mrs. Z walked behind me and lightheartedly asked, "What happened to my apple cider at noon?"

"I'm sorry," I quickly answered. "I thought you wouldn't be back for a few days."

"Oh, we took care of everything. Today is a day for new beginnings."

"Mrs. Z, have you seen Anna, the maid from the north wing?"

"No, I haven't. How are you, Edgar?"

"I'm fine, except for my back."

"Have you seen my son?"

"No, ma'am. He and Ms. Rose did not come home last night."

Mrs. Z looked puzzled. "Where could they be?" she mumbled.

Then the door opened, and it was Kendrick and Rose. I looked at Mrs. Z. She smiled and looked relieved.

Mr. Z came in a few seconds behind them. "Son, have you made up your mind? The police are on their way."

"What are you talking about, Father?"

"If you have to ask—well, you did not make the right decision."

"I made myself clear to you when we were cutting sugarcane yesterday."

"So stubborn. Why can't you be more like your cousin Thomas? Love—love is nothing when you are not connected to the right, pure person. I do everything for you."

"We do it all," Mrs. Z said.

"All the things that cause other people to look away," Mr. Z added. "Do you think having all this was handed to me? Hell, no! I had to earn it, like my true name, Kend. You know this, and that is why I didn't give you my name. Kendrick, nothing was given to me. You, with your sissy-ass picture-taking. Don't you know that we cannot have any stains in our circle? The help—it's their job; otherwise, they would not be here either. Choose now, son!"

"Father, I have chosen, and I married the woman with whom I decided to live my life—in a shack or under a bridge or in a field of impossible dreams. Love—true, pure love—will make it a home, anywhere and under any circumstances."

"I thought you once loved me, Father."

"Son," Mrs. Z interjected, "you have to understand where your Father and I come from."

"No, Mother, your roots are hateful and prejudiced. We will have no part of it. It is a shame that you will not be a part of your grandchildren's lives, but Rose and I do not want our children stained by your evil roots."

"I thought you said she was a virgin."

"I did; we both were. We've been married for five months. In six months, Lord willing, we will have twins."

"Son, I tried with you," Mr. Z said. "Who is going to take care of them while you are behind bars for murder? Your darkie wife is not getting one red cent of our money, nor will those half-breed bastards!"

"Father, I feel sorry for you and Mother."

"It is too late," Mr. Z said. "The police are here."

Kendrick looked at me and smiled. "No, Father, you and Mother are going away for murder. How could you both be so evil? Mother, you were the imaginary angel I talked to during all the years I was away at school. What happened?"

"What proof do you have?" his father asked, laughing and pushing Kendrick with his fist.

"Father, did you forget I used to take pictures?"

"So what? Edgar burned everything."

"No, Mr. Z," I corrected him. "I kept everything you ordered me to burn or throw away—for Kendrick. It's in the stable through the tunnel, in the corner, behind the fifth brick next to the hidden wine cellar, where you keep your rattlesnake poison."

"Guess all those years of school didn't cure your sissy-ass, picture-taking self," Mr. Z said to his son. Then he turned to me. "And you, you ragged-ass nigger, that is why I treat you and all the others the way I do. You cannot be trusted. I gave you all a place to sleep and paid off too many goddamn debts. Get out of my house! Just like I killed your gorilla-made parents and got away with it, this is no different. The one goddamn nigger I trusted betrayed me!"

"Kend, I know you and your wife knows that Rose is Sarah's great-granddaughter, so Rose is a Zlebra and the twins will be too."

"My lawyer is on his way," Mr. Z said.

Kendrick addressed the police who had come to his door. "Officers, these are the murderers. They both are on camera, throwing the maid Anna down the stairs last night. They put her body in the garbage bin behind the stables on the east side. If that is not enough proof for these murderers, they also killed a garden of Negros, Puerto Ricans, and Mexicans. Go dig them up. If you dig in those piles of dirt-covered boxes at the police station, you will see those buried bodies are the poor people who went missing."

Kendrick and I then looked at Mr. Z, saying together, "The less important."

CHAPTER 6

After Life's Storms

"Edgar, you will be taken care of," Kendrick told me. "My parents bought you, and you will get paid for your tormented years of slavery. I am so sorry."

"Don't worry, Edgar," Rose said. "His parents are in jail, and you will come live with us." She kissed me and added, "I hope you agree."

"I love you, Pops," Kendrick said, "because you are the only man who showed me how to be a man through kindness and love, when it should have my father, whose DNA I share. Instead, it was a black man named Edgar Robert, whom I dearly love like a father. All the things I didn't receive from my father, you selflessly granted to my hurting soul."

The estate was sold within five years. The local newspaper said that the buyer was some corporate organization. The developers made it into a hospital, hotel, and restaurant for the pure, rich white folk, with golf courses, horse racing, and a park for their kids.

The landscaping wasn't anything compared to what it was when I cared for it, but they had to dig up all those graves and restructure the ground. What was owned by one evil man now belonged to many evil men. We "less-important" were not allowed anywhere on the property; if we were caught on or near it, the law said it was OK to kill us. The staff were white, from the doctors down to the stable hands.

Little changes, in baby steps.

I moved to a little cabin in the back of Kendrick and Rose's wooden house that sat on three beautiful acres with a garden of English bluebells. All the ones who worked for the Zlebras got paid, and the dead family members finally had a resting place, even though it wasn't as beautiful as the east garden.

The senior Zelbras were sentenced to fifteen years each, but they only served two months because of a temporary illness, which went away the second they were released. That's what money gets you----less punishment in this life, but not the next one. They still had money, even after many lawsuits, but they never got an estate like they once had.

I cannot say that everybody lived happily ever after because I am haunted by so many evils and the cries of the innocent who were tortured and killed. My hand was to the shovel—the graves I dug for countless souls.

People like Kend and Frances were not bothered by the lives they had taken. It seemed that the more evil you were, the longer you lived.

But I know this: the Bible does not lie. Proverbs 14:11–12 says, "The house of the wicked shall be overthrown, but the tabernacle of the upright shall flourish. There is a way that seemeth right unto a man but the end thereof are the ways of death."

EPILOGUE

Baby steps that were seen through Edgar Robert's heart, before he let go of this life, were the petals told through the hearts of his nonbloodline grandchildren. He was the only grandfather they ever knew—a black slave who had taught their white father that love is deeper than color and more than DNA.

It was springtime, and everything had changed, including Kendrick and Rose Zlebra's last name. Their four children—Anna Marie Robert, Sarah Ann Robert, Kendrick Robert Jr., and Edgar Robert II—placed white lilies and blue roses around their grandfather Edgar Robert's grave; he had lived to the ripe old age of 102. He was a good man, and God blessed him to see rainbows of beauty, with his heart bursting in love with his family, after enduring a lifetime of darkness and hate. Now, he was surrounded by a bed of English bluebells and a field of flowers two miles wide.

Mr. and Mrs. Zlebra's hearts stopped beating twenty-four hours after Edgar Robert closed his peaceful eyes. Their gravesite was somewhere on the flowerless lot where the less-important, unnamed burial grounds were located.

Printed in the United States
By Bookmasters